Dear Parent:

Congratulations! Your child is taking the first steps on an exciting journey. The destination? Independent reading!

STEP INTO READING® will help your child get there. The program offers five steps to reading success. Each step includes fun stories and colorful art. There are also Step into Reading Sticker Books, Step into Reading Math Readers, Step into Reading Phonics Readers, Step into Reading Write-In Readers, and Step into Reading Phonics Boxed Sets—a complete literacy program with something for every child.

Learning to Read, Step by Step!

Ready to Read   Preschool–Kindergarten
• big type and easy words • rhyme and rhythm • picture clues
For children who know the alphabet and are eager to begin reading.

Reading with Help   Preschool–Grade 1
• basic vocabulary • short sentences • simple stories
For children who recognize familiar words and sound out new words with help.

Reading on Your Own   Grades 1–3
• engaging characters • easy-to-follow plots • popular topics
For children who are ready to read on their own.

Reading Paragraphs   Grades 2–3
• challenging vocabulary • short paragraphs • exciting stories
For newly independent readers who read simple sentences with confidence.

Ready for Chapters   Grades 2–4
• chapters • longer paragraphs • full-color art
For children who want to take the plunge into chapter books but still like colorful pictures.

STEP INTO READING® is designed to give every child a successful reading experience. The grade levels are only guides. Children can progress through the steps at their own speed, developing confidence in their reading, no matter what their grade.

Remember, a lifetime love of reading starts with a single step!

Visit us on the Web!
StepIntoReading.com
randomhouse.com/kids

Educators and librarians, for a variety of teaching tools, visit us at RHTeachersLibrarians.com

ISBN 978-0-449-81878-7 (trade) — ISBN 978-0-449-81879-4 (lib. bdg.)

Printed in the United States of America

10 9 8 7 6 5 4 3 2 1

STEP INTO READING®

STEP 2

nickelodeon

DORA the EXPLORER

Tea Party in Wonderland

Adapted by Delphine Finnegan

Based on the teleplay "Dora Through the Looking Glass"
by Chris Gifford

Illustrated by Victoria Miller

Random House 🏠 New York

Dora loves reading
to Boots
and the kitties.
They are reading
<u>Alice in Wonderland</u>.

Knock, knock.

No one is at the door.

No one is at the window.

<u>Knock, knock.</u>

It is the mirror!

The mirror is magic!

The kitties jump

into the mirror.

They chase a rabbit
into Wonderland.
"Hurry! The Queen
is waiting
at her tea party,"
says the rabbit.

Dora and Boots
must find the kitties.
They follow them
into the mirror.

Dora and Boots
are in Wonderland!
The kitties are
still chasing the rabbit.

They go down
a rabbit hole.

Dora and Boots are too big!

Map can help.

They need to sail

to the giant trees,

pass the tiny animals,

and go through a forest.

They need a boat.

The Mad Hatter can help.

He makes magical hats.

He turns a hat
into a boat!

They sail away
to the giant trees.

How will Dora and Boots
get through the trees?

They reach and swing
from vine to vine.
They make it
through the maze
of trees!

They meet a Bandersnatch.

He has hurt his toes.

Dora gives him bandages.

The Bandersnatch
thanks them with a ride.
They must find
the tea party
and the kitties.

Tiny animals
block the way.
"Can we pass by?"
Dora asks.
The animals make way
for Dora and Boots.

They still need to find
the kitties.
They head
to the forest.

In the forest,
people forget
who they are.
People forget
where they are going.

A fluffy cat tells Dora
and Boots to remember.

They sing a song.

It helps them remember.

"Dora, Boots,

kitties, tea party."

They sing it over and over.

The song works!

Dora and Boots

do not forget.

The forest door opens.

They find the tea party!
But they must watch out
for the Queen!
She is mean!

The rabbit arrives
with the kitties.

He has the Queen's tarts.

The Knave of Hearts wants
to take them.

Dora stops him.

Everyone cheers for Dora except the Queen.

Dora tells the Queen
about the helpful friends
in Wonderland.
The Queen agrees
to be kind.

Tarts for everyone!